CHRISTMAS Tree Connection

ELLE RUSH

Elle Rush

For Ross, my partner in all things and that goes double for my Christmas obsession.

And in memory of my Dad. The firsts are always the hardest.

CHAPTER 1

*N*ovember 1971
December, Manitoba, Canada (a two-hour drive north of Grand Forks, North Dakota)

Adelaide North had to wait twenty more minutes before she could have lunch, and she knew for a fact that there was a container of her famous, mouthwatering coconut Christmas trees available for all the tellers in the break room. She hoped her coworkers' generous holiday spirits had left her some, especially since she was the most junior staff member at the branch, which meant she got the late lunch shift.

Most of the time, she didn't care when she ate. Not missing out on the cookies was her biggest concern. Besides, there were a few benefits to the late lunch shift, like serving the man waiting in line. Not the dude she was currently dealing with; the handsome, tall, blond one who was three people back. She hoped he came to her wicket.

Adelaide took her rubber date stamp, punched it onto the

red ink pad, and smacked it against the deposit book page, confirming the deposit that Greg George had just made into his "Christmas by George" business account. "You opened your tree lot a week early this year, Mr. George," she noted as she pushed the deposit book back under the plastic window.

Greg insisted on being called "Mr. George" when he came into the bank, even though they had been in school together. She hated doing it, but a job was a job. "Thank you, Adelaide," he said, stressing her first name. "I had to get a jump on the competition. At least for this year. I don't think the new North Pole lot will be around for long." His second comment was a little louder, meant to carry to the other customers in the bank. "After all, Christmas By George is a local landmark."

She valiantly fought off a snicker. Calling the seasonal business a landmark was stretching it. While it was true that the Georges had served up Christmas trees to the community for the last few years, it wasn't as if their tree lot had been around for decades. Greg's father had rented a barren property on the edge of town and brought in trees to sell. Adelaide wasn't even sure that the Georges would be the guaranteed victor in a holiday battle considering how many bad vibes Greg had generated with his attitude since he'd taken it over three years earlier. "Can I do anything else for you, Mr. George?" she asked, crossing her fingers for a no.

"Actually, yes. I was wondering if you wanted to get rid of any of your little Christmas ornaments. They didn't seem to be selling very well at the craft show on the weekend. I could do you a favour and take them off your hands. They might be good enough to give away as a free gift with purchase. What do you say? I'd be willing to go as high as a dollar each."

She sputtered, too incoherent to immediately reply. Her

little ornaments as he called them sold like hotcakes at five dollars apiece at the Morris community craft show. His generous offer also didn't address the fact that each one cost her a dollar and a half to make. She wasn't breaking the bank with her profits, but Greg's offer was an insult. "I did just fine at the craft show, Mr. George, so I'll keep selling them myself, thank you very much. Do you have the branch's number to call in your coin orders?" she asked.

"Your loss. And yes, I do have the number, Adelaide," he confirmed. He slowly inserted his deposit book into the canvas cash bag. "I'll see you on Thursday morning."

Adelaide willed him to hurry up. The other tellers on duty had taken a customer each, leaving one at the front of the row. Finally, Greg George stepped aside, and she leaned forward. "Hi, Victor. I can help you over here."

All the tellers had favourite customers. Victor Klassen was hers. Not because he was unfailingly polite whenever he was in the bank. Or because he always cleaned her windshield when she filled her tank at the local gas station. Or even because he was the cutest single guy in December. He had something she couldn't put her finger on, and that something left her dying to find out the rest of his secrets.

But she'd never have the opportunity to learn what they were if she couldn't get past his shyness. Victor could meet her eye and had mastered small talk, but the blue-eyed Viking of a man never said a word about himself. Adelaide had tried every weapon in her flirting arsenal. She'd struck out with conversations about hockey and football, television shows, camping and provincial parks, and pizza. She was running out of topics.

As she separated and counted dollar bills for the gas station's deposit, she kept sneaking glances at Victor. He didn't look well. His dark blond hair was plastered to his forehead with a sheen of sweat, and he looked pale under the bank's fluorescent lights. "Are you feeling okay, Victor?"

"I'm just nifty. I heard what Greg said. It wasn't true. I saw how busy you were at the craft show. I know people went bananas for your stained glass ornaments."

"Thank you for that."

When he gulped down air, Adelaide got seriously worried. "Are you sure you're fine?"

"Actually, I need to ask you something."

Her breath caught. This was it! Victor was finally going to ask her out. "Yes?" And *yes!* she thought.

"I was wondering," he paused, swallowing hard, "if you'd like to have coffee with me tonight. If you didn't have any plans. I know it's last minute and you're probably busy and—"

"I'm free," Adelaide interrupted. Technically, she had a hot date on television with a rumpled detective in an overcoat and a murder victim, but Columbo placed a distant second behind Victor.

His sigh of relief was audible. "Thank you. My grand-mother thought you'd be a good choice. The garage closes at seven. Can I meet you at Nell's Cafe at eight?"

Adelaide was stuck on the mention of his grandmother. Did he think they needed a chaperone? "Sure?"

"Great! I knew you could help. I'll see you tonight."

Now she was helping him with something? That didn't sound like a date. What had she gotten herself into? "See you then, Victor."

Her co-worker Martha tapped her on the shoulder as she returned, signaling that Adelaide was free to take her own lunch. Adelaide stamped Victor's deposit book, put up her

"Next Teller Please" sign, and locked her cash drawer. As she sat in the break room, she replayed their conversation in her head and realized that Victor had never said the word "date." She'd assumed. "A-S-S-U-M-E," Adelaide said aloud as she filled in 18 Across on the newspaper's daily crossword.

At least she could get the puzzle right.

CHAPTER 2

*H*e'd done it. He'd asked Adelaide North out on a date. She was by far the prettiest girl in December with her stunning auburn hair and deep brown eyes. It was too bad he'd never have a chance with her. She wouldn't be hanging around their small town for much longer; smart, funny girls like her always headed to the big city to find their fame and fortunes. He, on the other hand, was determined to achieve the same degree of success in his hometown.

He'd better; he'd been planning to run his own business since he was twelve. Victor had spent half his life getting North Pole Evergreens ready to launch, and that time had finally arrived. He first got the idea to own his own Christmas tree farm during the holiday season the year he turned twelve. He started doing odd jobs and saving his money for it when he turned thirteen. The day after his eighteenth birthday, he bought a parcel of land south of Winnipeg. That same summer he planted his initial set of evergreen seedlings. Seven years later, he was ready to harvest his first crop of Christmas trees. He couldn't fail now.

Victor just needed a little help crossing the finish line. He had a feeling that Adelaide was the person to do it. Four days from now, when he held North Pole Evergreens' Grand Opening, he needed to make a gigantic splash. He had to crush, not just compete with, Christmas by George. Eight years ago when he had his idea, there hadn't been a single Christmas tree seller in December. Then five years ago, the Georges had opened their tree lot, *after* he had already committed all his savings to his future business.

Adelaide Klassen's artistic ornaments could provide a huge draw to the lot. He knew exactly what he wanted to ask her to do. He'd refined his proposal endlessly over the two days in between customers at his day-job at the local gas station. All he needed to do was convince her that he was the man for her before Greg beat him to it.

Nell's Café was a small restaurant, not more than a hole-in-the-wall with a dozen tables, attached to the December Motor Inn. The motel usually had several vacant rooms, but it filled up on holidays or when the RCMP closed the highway to North Dakota during winter blizzards. Locals kept the café in business in the between times.

Adelaide was already there, nursing a large hot chocolate with an even larger cloud of whipped cream on top. Locks of her red hair kept escaping from where she tucked them behind her ear whenever she bent her head to work on a crossword puzzle. It wasn't just a *TV Guide* crossword either; it was a big one. And she was completing it in pen. As soon as she saw him, she dropped her pen in the crease of the puzzle book and closed it, giving him her complete attention. "Hi, Victor."

"Hi. Can I get you a brownie?" He'd been hoping to butter her up by covering the tab, but since she already had her drink, the least he could do was spring for a treat to go with it. The favour he was fishing for was huge. The brownie was a bribe just for the privilege of asking for it.

"Sure."

He shouldn't be so nervous. He'd known Adelaide for years. They'd even taken a night class together at the high school. It had been on how to set up a small business. They hadn't spoken about their private projects, but he and Adelaide had discussed all the information the visiting instructor had provided.

"Is your grandmother okay?" she asked once he'd taken his seat across from her.

"What?"

"You said that your grandma thought I'd be a good choice. Does she need my help with something? I'm not sure what I can do, but I'd be happy to talk to her."

"No, Gran is fine, thanks. We were at the craft show in Morris last Saturday and we saw your table with all your stained glass ornaments." Ornaments was too small of a word for what Adelaide created. Her Christmas tree decorations could fit in the palm of his hand, but whether they were flat or 3-D, they were all works of art. Bright, patterned Christmas balls looked like they'd been cut from the Eaton's catalogue. Candy canes of tiny, alternating red and white boxes had hung from the tiny tree in the display, catching the light from all directions. Her masterpiece had been a funky, multi-layered wreath of leaves in various greens garnished by frosted white berries and protruding, cheery, red poinsettias. "They were really pretty."

Her brown eyes crinkled in confusion. "Thanks?"

Victor sighed. He needed to stop getting distracted by Adelaide's eyes and get to the point. "Do you remember when we took that night class together? I was working on a business plan, but I never told you what it was for. I own a Christmas tree farm. I've owned it for seven years, but this is the first season that it will be open to the public."

"You're selling Christmas trees? Cool! What's your farm called?"

"North Pole Evergreens. And I'm not just selling trees. I'm growing my own."

"It's the whole experience? Are you saying people can come out and choose and cut their own trees rather than just pick a pre-cut one? They'll love that."

Adelaide understood his vision. Somehow, he knew she would. "I'll have some pre-cut ones, of course, but yes. Customers can choose and cut their own trees from designated areas. I have fire-pits and hay bales for seats. It's a whole Christmas destination. At least it will be some day." He had plans but he had to start with step one, which was selling enough North Pole evergreens to turn a profit so he could reinvest in the company.

And to do that, he had to have a successful launch. "My grand opening is this coming weekend. My dad was able to cut me a deal on advertising, so I have ads running in this week's Beausejour Beaver, Steinbach Carillon and Morden Times. I've also sprung for a small one in the Winnipeg Free Press. But every other tree lot in the province is advertising too. I need a draw, so people choose my tree lot over all the others in the area. Something special. I think your ornaments would be the perfect thing to attract them. They were the best thing at the show."

A smile exploded across her face. "Thank you! That's very

flattering. I'm proud of them. Even if they didn't sell as well as I might have told some people." Her grin faltered.

"You should be proud. They're gorgeous. They're art." She recovered some of her smile, and Victor wondered if he was the first to pay her creations such compliments. "Unfortunately for me, they're also beyond my budget for what I'd like to do."

"Which is?"

"Have an already decorated tree filled with them to raffle off to customers." He could picture it in his head. He saw a beautifully lit evergreen, garland woven around the tree, with glittering glass ornaments hanging off the ends of the branches. The whole thing would glow from the inside with hundreds of Christmas lights. It wouldn't be as shiny as the new aluminum Christmas trees that were all the rage, but it would still look wonderful. "I can't get as many as I want, but I was wondering, and I hope you're not insulted—" he crossed his fingers under the table—"if I ask whether you would do any kind of discount on a dozen ornaments." Twelve of Adelaide's creations wouldn't fill a tree, but he could highlight them and use complimentary plain ones to fill the rest of the space. "I overheard Greg offering to buy them but—"

She raised her hand, cutting him off. "Greg's offer is absolutely not under consideration," she interrupted. "I love the idea of a Christmas tree family afternoon, Victor. I'd help you out just to get one over on Greg, but I think you can do better than me selling you a dozen. Would you be willing to let me look at your space, and we'll see what ideas we can come up with?" Adelaide asked.

He nodded eagerly. He was dying to show off North Pole Evergreens to somebody he wasn't related to. His father had worked for the local paper his entire life, earning his way from a junior advertising sales rep to the editor, but his dad was very much a company man. He didn't understand why his son would want to risk everything on his own business. Victor couldn't explain how the idea of building an entire company himself made him feel excitement, not fear. "Today was my last day at the garage until the new year. I'm taking the last half of November and all of December off to give the lot my full attention. When works for you?"

She smiled. "Tomorrow right after work? We should be able to get out there while it's still light," she suggested.

"Great. It's a date."

Then she smiled even bigger.

CHAPTER 3

*I*t was a typical Manitoba winter so far. When Adelaide awoke, a fresh dusting of snow covered the world. It had snowed once in the last week of October but that had melted before Halloween. That had been followed by two weeks of overcast skies and cold winds. But the bracing cold that morning told her that winter was now here to stay. She reluctantly retired her dress boots for the season and pulled out her heavy winter boots with their thick felt liners for her walk through the woods after work.

Victor was waiting for her when she left the bank at four o'clock. "Do you want to drive with me or follow me out with your car?" he asked.

"I'll follow you." It would give her a chance to check out the signage for his tree farm. She'd paid extra attention to the marketing section of their night class and wanted to know if Victor had taken those lessons to heart.

He had. He'd set up a large sandwich board just off the highway. **North Pole Evergreens Christmas Tree Farm, Fridays 4pm to 8pm, Saturdays and Sundays 12pm to 8pm.**

Adelaide nodded in approval. It was clear, easy to read, and had a two-foot tree attached to the side to illustrate the product.

But that was nothing compared to the fab wooden sign Victor had erected at the turn-off to his tree farm. The carved wood displayed the company name and had hanging boards announcing each of the sets of hours, plus a spare indicating there would be "Family Fun" and "Fire Pits". The whole thing was bracketed with 3D trees popping out of the frame. Victor had also wired lights over the top of the sign to illuminate it in the dusk and early winter darkness. She whistled. "A-plus for signage, Victor," she said to herself.

The gravel road twisted out of sight from the highway, but soon it opened into a large, clearing. A small trailer with a picnic table in front was parked at the far end. Strings of outdoor lights spread like a spiderweb to poles surrounding an area filled with sawhorses. She imagined that was where pre-cut trees would be stacked. Adelaide counted three fire pits, each with its own foot-high corrugated metal frame. The final item of note was an outhouse hiding behind the trailer.

She parked beside Victor's classic truck. "Give me the tour!" she exclaimed.

Victor walked her around the clearing. He grabbed her hand when she tripped over a rough patch hidden under a snow drift. He let her go as soon as she found her feet. "This will be my pre-cut area. I'm only having four sections this year. Medium and large trees, white spruce and balsam fir," Victor said. "I kept things pretty simple for my first couple plantings. I didn't start to expand until my third year. Want to see where people can chop down their own trees?" he asked, reaching for her hand again before she had a chance to answer.

"Definitely," Adelaide said with a laugh as he pulled her down a path cut through the brush. Pine boughs and branches from cleared birch and poplar trees lined the way. In the dimming light, the green trees began to take on a blue hue, reflecting the darkening sky.

"I'll be spreading hay to walk on," Victor said. "It will ensure people don't go to the wrong sections by mistake. Here are this year's trees. Two hundred and fifty of the finest live Christmas trees that southern Manitoba has to offer." Row after row of perfectly shaped evergreens stretched out in front of her.

"I've also arranged for The Fry Guys food truck to come on opening weekend. It will give people a reason to hang around longer, which means more chances for them to buy accessories like your ornaments, right?"

"Definitely. You are going to rock this," she told him. Victor's set-up was excellent. It was similar to every other Christmas tree lot she'd ever been to, but better. It was almost like she could feel his pride and excitement in the place. "Speaking of my stained glass, what did you want to do with it?"

"Come on." He dragged her back to the trailer. "I have a spotlight, and I want to shine it on a tree outside the door, right here. The spotlight would highlight your ornaments, and I could keep an eye on them. What do you think?"

As flattered as she was by Victor's excitement, Adelaide wasn't sold on the idea. Her ornaments were accents, not the whole show. "Honestly, I'm afraid they'd get lost on a tree, especially outdoors. Blowing snow and dirt would obscure the shine from the glass quickly."

His shoulders slumped. "You hate the idea."

"No, not at all. I've just been working with stained glass for a long time and know what works. Would you be interested in a tree-shaped rack that you could display them on?" she asked.

"Do you think that would draw enough attention?"

"It would if there were fully decorated trees nearby to show off your product. You could put one of your amazing signs by the rack saying that people could enter to win a dozen ornaments of their choosing if they bought a tree."

"Wouldn't I have the same visibility problem with the other trees? How would I decorate them so that they can stand up out in the elements?"

"I'd do it by colour." Adelaide pulled him back a few steps. "Picture it. A primo tree with white lights and all silver decorations on one side, and another with red lights and all red decorations on the other. Maybe some freshly fallen snow on their branches. Sister evergreens of Yuletide beauty."

She grabbed his shoulders and turned him until he faced the path running to the cut-it-yourself rows. "You could also have another pair of lit trees marking the area that you are using this year, if you can get power to them. If you can't, you can just have decorated ones at the end of that trail. Reinforce the idea of the need for ornaments. You can do it all for cheap if you get the big containers of plastic ones from Woolco or Eaton's." She could imagine families coming out to revel in nature but being wowed by a little human sparkle. Kids would be stoked wanting to get home to decorate their own trees.

"I really wanted to use your ornaments, though," Victor said. "My grandma has *Good Housekeeping* and *Chatelaine* magazines all over her house, so I know how stately that mono-coloured trees can look. But your art is special."

He wasn't humouring her. He meant it. She could tell. "Thank you for that. Truly. I'd love to find a way to make it work for you."

"I'll look at your display rack if you think that's best."

Another idea popped into her head, and her jaw dropped at the audacity of it. It would kill three birds with one stone. She could sell her ornaments, prove Greg George wrong, and give Victor the art display he wanted. But her idea would make it about her and not him. She'd find another way.

She mustn't have hidden her reaction very well, because Victor squeezed her mittened hand. "What, Addy?" he asked.

"I had an idea, but I'm afraid it would take away from your family Christmas tree experience rather than add to it."

"How about you let me decide that."

Adelaide took a deep breath. "What would you think if I set up a table here this weekend to sell my stained glass, in addition to the prize display?"

He nodded slowly. "I'd like to hear more, but I'm freezing. Would you like to come in for a cup of cocoa and we can discuss it out of the wind?"

Victor's hopeful look made her nod.

He grinned, and fished a set of keys out of his coat pocket. "It'll take a minute to get the heater going but the trailer warms up quickly." A few clicks later, the propane heater opposite the small folding table in the kitchen rumbled to life and began pumping out hot air. He ran to his truck and returned with a jug of water, which he poured into a waiting pot on the two-burner stove-top. Then he plugged in a small appliance and more warmth filled the room. "It's a car interior heater," he explained when he noticed her staring at the counter.

"That's not what I'm looking at." Adelaide pulled off a glove and picked up an exquisitely carved wooden drum that fit in her palm. "What's the skinny on this?"

"Nothing." He reached for it, but she pulled her hand away.

"Funny, it looks like a Christmas tree ornament." She scanned the counter and found a thumb-sized Santa face with a tall hat and a long beard. Then she spotted a half-carved star peeking out from under a rag. "Victor Klassen, you've been holding out on me. You're an artist too."

"No, I was just fooling around when I had extra time on my hands. That's all scrap wood."

"This is not scrap," she protested. "Have you made more than ten?" When his face suddenly turned red, her jaw dropped. "More than a hundred? Two hundred?" Victor could be sitting on a goldmine. She wasn't about to let them all go to waste.

"Maybe not two hundred," he hedged.

"Listen up, Victor. If you decide that I can set up a table with my stained glass this weekend, you can bet your wooden ones are going to be taking up half the space. Lucky for you, I have more than one display rack."

"I couldn't. My carvings are nothing like your ornaments."

"Thank goodness," Adelaide told him. "We don't want them to be the same. Stained glass and carved wood will appeal to totally different buyers. Speaking of buyers, do you realize that you get to keep all the profits from your ornament sales? Tell me that selling twenty dollars' worth of carvings that you've already made and are just sitting around doesn't sound like a good bonus every weekend."

"It sounds very good. I'd happily take an extra hundred dollars a season," Victor said as he scooped hot chocolate mix into the pot.

"How many of those can you make a year? A hundred?"

"Not quite that many. But I've been coming here for years. I have a stockpile." He poured the cocoa into a mug and set it on the table, then slipped into the bench across from her.

"Do you think that an ornament table and some decorated Christmas trees will be enough of a draw to bring people over from Christmas by George?" Adelaide asked.

She jumped when he gave a low growl. "I can't bear the thought of losing to Greg because his company has a five-year head start when he doesn't even grow his own trees."

"You won't lose. I think we're just getting started on what North Pole Evergreens can do. You open this coming weekend, right?"

Victor nodded, his blue eyes blazing. "Right."

"Then we still have tomorrow night to get your plans in motion."

"Will one night be enough?"

"If we do it right, one night is all we need."

CHAPTER 4

*V*ictor was spending his third evening in as many days on yet another date with Adelaide North. Christmas had come early this year and Santa had been very good to him. At least, that's how it felt. This time, they'd arranged for Victor to pick her up from her apartment building after work.

Adelaide had brought along a backpack, which she pulled into her lap as soon as they hit the highway. "I did some research when I got home last night. I think you have some money-making opportunities that Greg simply can't offer. I'll need to check the prices in a craft store, but if I'm right, I found something that will only cost you about five dollars in supplies, a few buckets that can be reused, and some time." She stopped short and turned her head to stare at him. "That is, if you want to hear another idea."

Victor nodded vigorously. His old red pick-up could barely contain her energy. Who was he to stop her when she was on a roll. "I absolutely want to hear all your ideas. What is it?"

Adelaide waved a magazine in his face. "Wreaths and natural décor are the in things right now. According to the article in here, you are literally throwing money away. I saw it with my own two eyes."

"I am not."

"You are too," she argued. "You need to use your tree lot to accessorize your trees."

She was full of energy, but not making any sense. "I thought that was what this trip to the city was for. I'm not wasting anything." Victor was preserving every tree he could if it wasn't big enough to cut down this year so he could use it next season.

"No, we're still buying decorations. You want Christmas *accessories*, to bring the outdoors into your customers' homes. Or the indoors out. I'm not sure which. You need to put all those pine boughs and skinny birch trees that you threw to the side as waste to good, profitable use."

"Those scrawny things? They aren't even big enough to be useful firewood. What do you propose we do with them?"

She held up a full-page photo. Victor waited for a break in traffic, and then glanced over. Then he looked again. The picture was of the exterior of a grand home: specifically of four steps leading to a landing in front of a double front door with matching sidelights. On the ends of the bottom steps, and at the base of each window were bushy displays of Christmas greenery with bright pops of shiny cranberry red. "How are we supposed to manage something like that?"

"You already have most of the big pieces we need. We arrange your clearing discards artfully in a pail, wrap them with twine and red ribbon to hold them in place, then fill the pail with water. Once it freezes, we take them out, wrap the base in burlap, tie it closed with more ribbon and twine, and *voilá*! You have a festive outdoor decoration with a built-in base for your porch or front step. Cost to you, ribbon, twine and burlap. Value to your customers, priceless."

"It can't be that simple."

"That's what you want your customers to think. Even if you discount them with a tree purchase, you're still making money. I'll bet Christmas by George isn't offering anything like that," Adelaide crowed.

"I doubt they are either." It was a pretty far out idea. Victor didn't think anybody would be interested in buying something like that from him either, but as Adelaide had pointed out, it would only cost him a few dollars to try her idea. If he sold a handful of his wooden carvings, it would pay for the supplies and at the very worst he'd come out even. "Will we have to stop at another store?"

"Just one."

They settled in for the drive. The more Victor thought about Adelaide's suggestions for North Pole Evergreens, the more he started to like them. She had an amazing head for business. But he wondered why she had all these ideas for his company and hadn't started her own yet. "If you get enough sales, are you looking to turn your stained glass art into a full-time job?"

"No. It's just a hobby."

That made sense, but it didn't answer the questions he had. "If that's not why you took the night class, what was it for?" he pressed.

She busied herself stuffing magazines back into her knapsack.

He groaned. "Come on, Addy. You've seen all the inner workings of my future Christmas tree empire. What was

23

your business plan for? Interior design? Professional holiday decorating company?"

Her cheeks turned bright red, and Victor realized it was from embarrassment and not from the heaters blowing hot air on her face full blast. "My dream is to have my own publishing company that produces Aunt Addy's Activity Books. You know, puzzle books with crosswords and search words and mazes and jokes and colouring pages." Then she sighed. "I have huge plans. I want to set up an annual subscription service that offers a new activity book mailed out each quarter. In Aunt Addy's fantasyland, I'd also have them for sale at every campground convenience store between Kenora and Calgary."

"That sounds amazing. Why haven't you? Don't you have enough puzzles?"

Adelaide burst into laughter. "Not enough? I have binders full of puzzles. *Binders*," she emphasized. "The content isn't the problem. It's trying to find a printer that's a bummer. I haven't been able to locate one who print only as many as I want. Seriously, what am I going to do with five thousand copies of the same activity book? I need somebody who will do small runs. Unfortunately, the cost is prohibitive. And that's just the first problem. I can't even think about distribution until I have something to distribute."

"Aunt Addy's Activity Books?" he repeated. That suited Victor's image of her right down to the ground. Smart and fun and always surprising. "I loved stuff like that when I was a kid. They were a godsend on road trips."

"Right?" she agreed. "I'm sure I could make it work if I could just find a printer. I have a summer adventures one ready to go. And a Christmas themed book already laid out." She sighed. "Right now, I'm stuck at the starting gate." She smiled at him, but he could see the disappointment behind it. "But tonight is about North Pole Evergreens and its associated, amazing accessories for all your interior and exterior decorating needs. Let's get shopping."

"I'm ready."

He had not been ready.

They went to the city's only mall; it had dozens of shops, all under one roof. First, they hit the department store at the north end. By the time Victor had chosen two colours of outdoor Christmas lights and grabbed two extension cords from the temporary Christmas display area, Adelaide was back with a shopping cart overflowing with ornament containers. "Addy, I thought we were only doing four trees."

"We aren't buying all of these."

"Thank goodness." She had to have over a dozen sets in various colours.

"They're your trees. I wanted to give you all the options. I personally like the silver and the gold. I'm not a fan of the pink and purple, but they have a huge selection so they must be fashionable colours this year. I'm not certain how green would look on a green tree, but I'm not dismissing it out of hand. We also have red and blue. What do you think?"

The purple was out. He didn't want one of his trees to look like they'd been decorated with grapes. He wasn't sold on the blue either. "Let's try the green." In a worst-case scenario, he'd spent five bucks on ornaments that he'd sell in a garage sale the next summer. "Green and silver trees in one location, red and gold in the other." Adelaide had shown him more pictures from her magazines in the parking lot, and he'd been drawn to the new style of blue lights with silver ornaments. He thought it might work well with green as well. The red and gold trees would have traditional multi-coloured lights.

"Come on, the craft store is at the other end of the mall."

Holiday banners hung from one side of the central corridor to the other, letting customers walk under a wonderland of swoops of fake greenery and Christmas lights. Tinny speakers piped peppy children singing peppier Christmas carols on an endless loop as Adelaide led him through the crowds toward their destination.

She paused in the mall's centre court. "There isn't a line for photos with Santa at the moment."

"So?"

"We should do it!"

Victor stopped dead, causing a woman carrying bags of shoeboxes to whack into him. "What? Why? We're adults."

"So what? Let's do it anyway," she repeated. "A photo with Santa would be fun. We can frame it for your trailer and call it "Preparations for North Pole Evergreens Grand Opening, 1971." It'll be for posterity, for after you become an international conglomerate."

"A conglomerate based on Christmas trees?"

"Think big," she encouraged.

"Still, and I repeat, we're adults."

"It'll be terrific advertising. Santa-endorsed Christmas trees." She grabbed his hand and began pulling him past the stuffed reindeer. "Santa, can my friend and I get our picture taken with you? We're planning an exciting Christmas decoration extravaganza, and we'd love a photo with you for inspiration."

"Ho, ho, ho! I think that's a terrific idea. Come on up." The jolly man in red heaved himself off his throne-like chair. He wrapped one arm around each of them.

Adelaide beamed. Victor dug deep and found a small smile to wear in the face of such ridiculousness. He supposed a little self-embarrassment was worth it to thank her for sacrificing her evening and helping him out.

"You can pick those up on the weekend," Santa said when one of his elves handed over a receipt for the photos.

"Thank you, Santa. Come on, Victor, we need to finish shopping."

She grabbed his arm again, and quickly got them to the craft store, where she became a bargain-hunting whirlwind. She directed him to the clearance corner, where she scooped end pieces of ribbon into her basket, then tossed rolls of jute twine and a raggedy partial bolt of burlap into her hand basket. "I think that's everything we needed for your birch and pine outdoor ice pots," she said. "Can you think of anything else?"

"I don't think that we need to buy more ornaments to add colour. We're going to have extras," Victor said. He was finally getting into the swing of things, especially after seeing a display similar to Adelaide's magazines when then entered the store.

"True. What do you think? Should we drive to another store and see if we can get different ornaments or better prices, or are you happy with what we have? If we head back now, you can get an early start on setting stuff up tomorrow in anticipation of your grand opening on Friday."

Victor didn't want their shopping trip to end but she was right. He needed every minute to prepare. "We should probably head home. I don't suppose that you're free tomorrow night, are you?" He'd already monopolized her all week; as much as he enjoyed spending time with Adelaide, his "small favour" had to be destroying her social life.

27

"I have something at seven thirty, but I'm free right after work until about seven. I can bring my table and ornaments, and we can work on some outdoor displays, if you want."

"That would be amazing." It killed him that he couldn't ask her out right then and there. It would sound like he was fulfilling an obligation to thank her for all her help. If he waited and asked her out after the grand opening, he could do it in good conscience and with the advantage of knowing a lot more about her. Victor wanted every edge he could get. "I'll see you tomorrow."

CHAPTER 5

*S*ometimes a girl got lucky. Like today. Not only had Greg George gone to one of the other tellers when he came in to make his deposit, he'd also walked out of the bank without his deposit bag. His loss was her gain. Adelaide helpfully told her manager that she'd be happy to drop off his deposit book after work, not out of the goodness of her heart but so she could sneak a peek at the competition.

Christmas By George was a pre-cut tree lot beside the gas station on the edge of town. Every year, they'd erect a snow fence around the perimeter and, like Victor, set up a small camper to act as an office. Usually, that was all there was to it.

Greg George had upped his game this year. He had a new sign with Christmas lights wrapped around it. The cheerful bulbs extended all around the fenced boundary. When she walked through the gate, Adelaide saw a small food trailer with "The Fry Guys" emblazoned on the side parked in the corner. That was not good news. She wondered if Victor knew.

Adelaide walked to the trailer and knocked on the metal door. "Hello? Greg?"

The door opened immediately. "Hi, Adelaide."

She held out the canvas bag. "Your deposit book."

"Thanks for the delivery. I appreciate you saving me the trip."

She blinked. She couldn't remember the last time Greg had said something nice to her. "You're welcome."

"Have you reconsidered my offer for your ornaments? You really want to get in with me early before I make the offer to somebody else. We're anticipating record sales this year."

"No, thanks. I need my whole inventory for my upcoming gig." She'd never sell out at Victor's tree farm, but every piece purchased would be worth five she'd give to Greg. "Are you having a food truck this weekend?"

"You bet. With complimentary hot chocolate. Our opening weekend went great but we need to keep up the momentum."

"That will be popular," she said honestly. "Be sure to call in your change order for the weekend before two tomorrow."

"I'll see you here for your tree," Greg said confidently before he closed the trailer door.

New lights to draw the eye. Free snacks. And a five-year head-start. Adelaide's heart sank on behalf of her new friend. Victor would have to hit it out of the park on opening weekend to establish his reputation as the place to go for Christmas trees against Greg's new and improved tree lot.

She continued down the highway. She first noticed that Victor had swept all the drifted snow away from his sandwich board sign, so it was clearly visible from the road. Then she saw that he'd brushed off the one at the turnoff too, as well as added bunches of small balloons so people couldn't miss it. He'd had a busy day.

When she parked, Adelaide was amazed at the rest of the transformation, and she thought that the lot had looked pretty good earlier in the week. A dozen trees were tied and leaning against the sawhorses, waiting for people who wanted to grab their pre-cut trees and go. Victor had already wrapped trees on either side of the trailer with blue bulbs. In the dimming evening light, they gave an unearthly glow to the green ornaments, but it was a unique effect. The silver ornaments also reflected the blue lights, creating a pair of stunning looks. Victor hadn't held back; he must have used every ornament in the boxes they bought, leaving no branch untouched. Adelaide approved. She hoped the trees would be enough to impress North Pole Evergreens' customers, so they raved louder than the people who went to Christmas by George.

"Thank God you're here, Addy!" Victor's red plaid jacket was loaded with pine needles, making him look like a massive porcupine. His hair was similarly spiky. From the way he was fidgeting, she figured he'd run his hands through it until it stood up by itself. "I have the pictures for your front step decoration thingies, but I can't get them to work. What am I doing wrong?"

His attempts looked like a bunch of broken branches stuck in a snow pile. She could see that he'd tried, but it was a disaster. Victor had done so well on everything else when it came to his tree lot, but his face when he looked at his creations made her feel like she'd kicked his puppy. "Hey, this is an experiment. Nothing ventured, nothing gained. Let me take a pass at it. I took a wreath- and cornucopia-making class this fall." She hoped the skills would transfer, or else Victor would have enough burlap to open a sack factory.

She gathered an armful of pine boughs and a pair of yard-long pieces of birch branch with bright white bark and began to stack them in a pile. When she was happy with how they looked, she wrapped the entire thing in twine to keep it steady, arranged the oversized branch bouquet in an empty bucket, then carefully lowered it to the ground. Adelaide held the branches steady while Victor filled the bottom third of the bucket with water. "Once it freezes, we'll add some red ribbon. What do you think?"

"It already looks better than mine," he said in relief. "You were right. If we have these on display, people will see them as they linger around the fire pits enjoying their snacks and drinks and grab one on the way out."

She gulped. He didn't know. Maybe she had the name wrong, and everything was fine. "You said you'd hired The Fry Guys truck to set up in your parking lot, right?"

"That's right."

"Have you confirmed with them lately?"

"No. They said they'd call on Friday at noon for directions." He focused his gaze on her face. "Why? Have you heard something?"

"I swung by Christmas by George on my way here to drop something off for Greg. And to spy. One of the things I spied was a Fry Guys truck already set up in his lot. He said that they were giving away free hot chocolate to his customers this weekend."

The look on Victor's face said it all. "What am I going to do?"

"Did you put "food truck" in your ads? Will people be expecting it?" Adelaide asked.

"No. It came together after the ads were designed, so it was supposed to be a surprise. I guess the surprise is on me. Are you sure?"

"I'm sure the trailer was parked there. I could see Greg hiring them out from under you. He's really upped his game this year. I think even the idea of North Pole Evergreens is causing him serious consternation. He may have some loyal customers, but he just can't offer the cut-your-own-tree experience. I think he's nervous." Greg had coasted on customer satisfaction for the last couple years, which wasn't hard when he was the only game in town. She'd heard about it in the bank. Any competition would be a dire threat. But so far, only she knew exactly what Victor had in store. Greg should be very worried.

"Then we're—you are," she stammered, "going to have to woo them and make them want to hang around without food," Adelaide said. "The firepits are great. Do you have a sound system set up?"

"Yes, but it's not much of one. It's just a turntable wired to some speakers on a post."

"It's better than nothing. Besides, you can't go wrong with Christmas carols. You do have the Partridge Family's Christmas album, right?" If he didn't have a copy of the new, best-selling holiday record in the country, there was going to be a riot. Mostly led by her.

"Um…"

"I'll lend you mine. For this weekend only. But you'd better have your own copy by next weekend." Victor was lucky she was willing to give up David Cassidy for three whole days.

"I'll get my own copy on Monday, I promise."

She breathed a double sigh of relief. First, that Victor

understood the musical sacrifice she was making in lending the album to him at all, and second, that he had decent taste in music.

"Let's get some more of these in buckets to freeze overnight. Then I have to go." She had a standing Thursday night businesswomen's meeting with Nell Grant, the owner of Nell's Cafe, Honey Allen, December's local make-up saleswoman, and Martha Martin, her fellow teller who also sold baked good at various local markets and weekend events around the province. For the first time in ages, she was going to have something to report about her own enterprises, including the fact that Victor had inspired her to start looking for a printer again.

An hour later, they had made five more arrangements. If Victor sold more than that on his opening evening, she'd be shocked. Thrilled for him, but shocked.

"Adelaide, thank you. I couldn't have done this without you. You're the bee's knees," he said as they stood beside her car while it warmed up. "I'm as ready as I can be for tomorrow." He let out a sigh that she could feel to her bones. "I just hope it will be enough."

Before she could talk herself out of it, Adelaide stepped forward, wrapped her arms around his waist and squeezed. It was a very squishy hug; their winter jackets had too much padding for her to put much force behind it, but it held all of her trust and encouragement. "It will be. We'll make sure of it."

CHAPTER 6

Friday dawned with a bright blue and cloudless sky, which meant that the November cold would be more intense than normal. Luckily, North Pole Evergreens was surrounded by trees to form a natural windbreak. Even so, Victor had three firepits ready to warm his hordes of happy customers. Or masses—he'd take masses of customers.

Honestly, he'd be thrilled with a dozen.

It was good to dream. While he was at it, he'd take a winning lottery ticket and a gift card to the best steakhouse in the province.

Victor smacked his hands together inside his thick, lined leather mittens to get the blood flowing. He had decided to err on the side of success and had cut and wrapped another eight trees for people who just wanted to grab and go. His assistant, his younger cousin Constantine Phelps, had raced out to help him as soon as school was out for the day. Constantine would be his right-hand man every weekend between now and Christmas. He had a full first aid kit and two fire extinguishers under the bench seats of the table in the trailer. He was ready. All he needed was the people.

The minute hand on his watch swept past the twelve so it was officially four o'clock. His eyes went to the road. Victor didn't expect anyone to be busting down his figurative front door the second that he opened for business, but it would have been nice. When nobody appeared after thirty seconds, he forced himself to turn away. "I need a fire," he called to Con. "Come take a break."

"It may be the only one we get today before people start arriving."

Victor appreciated his cousin's optimism.

He heard the first engine at half past four. Adelaide's old blue Mustang pulled around the corner and crept to the far end of the parking lot. She shouted as soon as she opened her door. "I brought a table and my ornaments. Can you help me carry them?"

Victor sprang into action. "We can put your table under the canopy." The small vinyl awning would provide a little protection against any snow that fell over the weekend. He also hoped that the idea of shelter would encourage people to look and linger a little longer.

"I also brought cookies. We'll need to keep our strength up as we run around filling orders all evening. I hope you like shortbread and coconut."

"Together?" Victor asked with trepidation. That sounded like a horrible combination.

"No! I have some rolled shortbread because it's not Christmas without shortbread. And for the more discerning palates, I have brought my famous coconut Christmas trees and coconut snowballs," she said.

"How on earth did you manage to make two batches of

cookies? You've either been at work or with me every day this week," Victor asked.

"I set my alarm for four-thirty this morning, so you had better be sure to tell me how good they are."

"They are the best cookies I've ever tasted in my life," he swore.

"You need to try them first."

"Nope. The answer will be the same."

She laughed. "Here, do me a solid and do not drop this. It's the cookies," Adelaide ordered as she carefully handed him a plastic container. She popped the trunk and hauled out a collapsible card table. On their second trip to her car, she handed him a large cardboard box, then grabbed a trio of wooden tree-shaped stands from her back seat and hip-checked the driver's door shut. "Let's get these set up."

She placed the stands on the table and secured their bases with beanbags made from Christmas-themed fabric. Then she filled the first with stained glass birds: bright red cardinals, cheery blue jays, white doves in singles and pairs. She loaded the second stand with glass candy canes, striped stockings, Santa faces and colourful Christmas balls hung from golden braids. Then she set up the third one and turned to him. "This one's yours. Where are your ornaments?"

"You know, two stands are more than enough selection for people," he hedged.

"Victor Middle-name-unknown Klassen, you go get your ornaments right now!"

"It's Nicolas," Constantine offered helpfully.

"Thanks!"

"It's like you want to get fired," Victor grumbled.

"Go ahead. You're the one who will have to explain it to my dad," his cousin said, backing away.

"I'm surrounded by traitors," Victor muttered as he stomped toward his trailer to get his box of hand carved ornaments. Maybe they weren't as terrible as he thought: Adelaide seemed to like them. But he couldn't imagine somebody paying good money for them.

Adelaide picked an assortment of his designs and hung them from the dowel branches. "Every one of these is money in your pocket. Remember that when you look at this table."

He hadn't sold a single tree yet. A dollar was starting to sound impressive.

The parking lot stayed empty until a little after five. He got excited when he heard an engine revving up the road from the highway. "Con, throw another log on the fire to get some flames going so it looks nice and warm. Adelaide—"

"The ornament table. I'm on it," she said, scurrying away from her hay bale.

His cousin warmed himself by the fire while Victor greeted his first customers, a couple from town who had brought their toddler with them. "Hi, I'm Brian Lewis, and my family tells me that we need a Christmas tree immediately if not sooner," the young dad said.

"Jilly is so excited," his wife said. "We know it's early, but she's promised to water it every day. If it's a little sparse by Christmas Eve, we'll add more decorations to hide the bare spots. What do you recommend?"

"The Balsam fir will hold its needles better, although the white spruce is bushier to start. Either way, I advise you to water it often, like you said, and try not to put it near a furnace vent or baseboard heater," Victor advised.

"Which ones are Balsam fir?"

Victor walked Brian over to the pre-cut tree stand, while Mrs. Lewis supervised the toddler, who was running around the open space. Victor was pleased to see that his cousin had moved to keep himself between the kid and the fire and had a close watch on the tiny tornado.

"Jeepers creepers! Jilly, come look at these," Victor heard the woman say. "They're just like the ones Poppa has on his tree at his house." He quickly glanced over his shoulder to see Mrs. Lewis pointing at his ornaments. Adelaide shot him a thumbs-up, and he turned his attention back to the husband.

"We have five-to-six-foot trees, and seven to eight. Do you know which would work better for your home?" Victor asked.

"We're in an apartment, so smaller is better. You're Victor Klassen, right? Your dad is the editor of the local newspaper?"

"Yep, we're those Klassens."

"He's the one who recommended your Christmas tree lot. I work for the company that prints the paper."

"That's cool!" Victor showed his first customer a couple of options, and then helped Brian load his six-foot balsam fir onto his roof rack. When they went to the office to make change, Victor offered Brian a ballot to win a dozen of Adelaide's ornaments. The guy groaned half-heartedly. "If I say no, my wife will kill me because she loves that stuff, even though our apartment is already bursting at the seams with Jilly's toys."

"Would you be willing to trade papers? A ballot for a business card?" Victor asked. "I have some printing questions and would love to have somebody local to ask."

"Absolutely."

When they came out, they found the wife fawning over the birch-and-pine buckets. "I know that we can't have one.

39

We don't have a balcony to put it on. But I'm definitely telling my folks about these. My mom will want one for her front steps. You're open tomorrow, right?"

"Saturdays and Sundays from noon till eight," Victor said.

"I'll let her know."

"Daddy, I got a Santa just like Poppa's!" The little girl bounced in glee. "Mommy says I can put it on the tree all by myself."

"Then we should get home and get the tree set up, don't you think?" The man shook his hand. "Thanks for helping me load this thing."

"Will you be okay at the other end?" Victor asked.

"Down is easier than up. And we have an elevator. Merry Christmas."

"You too," Victor said.

Adelaide came to stand beside him as they watched the family drive off. They'd just rounded the corner before he whirled around and hugged her. "First sale!"

"First two sales. She took one of your ornaments too," Adelaide said. She didn't pull away from his arms. Instead, she tilted her face up to his. "I told you this would work."

He didn't let her go. "We're going to do this."

"Yes, we are," she agreed.

"I'll bet you a kiss that you sell one of your ornaments to the next customer as well," he said, crossing his fingers inside his mitts that he wasn't misreading the look on her face.

Adelaide went up on her toes. "I'm willing to lose that bet now."

Her lips were warm against his in the cold evening air, and she tasted of hot chocolate and peppermint. When he pulled back, her brown eyes were sparkling, and her face was glowing from the Christmas lights strung overhead. He'd never forget how she looked in that moment.

Another car rumbled up the road. "Victor, more people!" Con yelled.

She grinned at him. "Let's do it again. The sales part now. The betting part later."

"You're on."

EPILOGUE

 ecember 1972

The Jackson 5 Christmas Album was an absolute hit. It was a couple of years old, but Adelaide was never in a million years going to get tired of "Santa Claus Is Comin' To Town." Unfortunately, Victor had put a one weekend moratorium on the album because Adelaide was playing it so often that even the customers noticed. She didn't care. She'd put that song on repeat at home.

Constantine stuck his head in the trailer. "We've had a request for some oldies from the big boss," he said as he snagged a coconut Christmas tree cookie.

"Groovy! Tell Victor that Bing Crosby and "White Christmas" are on the way," Adelaide said as she reached for a new album from their combined stack of records.

A lot of customers had commented on her music selections. She thought all the complaints and requests were terrific; it meant that North Pole Evergreens had a ton of people on the lot. She and Victor had started North Pole Evergreens' second year with a bang. A month later, they were still going gangbusters.

Last year, Victor's business had started out slow. Christmas by George had a terrific weekend with his hired food truck, while North Pole Evergreen had a slow but steady trickle of customers. But as soon as Greg George stopped offering free hot chocolate, the tide began to turn, especially when it was discovered that Greg's trees had been cut and bound weeks earlier. People coming to see Victor told stories of waking up in the morning to find half the tree's needles on the carpet with weeks to go before Christmas. Victor's cut-your-own fresh trees had been in high demand.

The door opened, letting a blast of cold air into the tiny trailer. The framed photo of Adelaide and Victor taken with Santa Claus the previous Christmas rattled in its place of honour on the wall. Victor stomped his boots on the mat at the door, then stepped inside. "It's brisk out there and it's starting to snow. I need you to warm me up," he said. Then he wrapped her in his arms and kissed her soundly before pressing his cold cheek to her warm one.

"I'll admit that you're cute, but I need to work. There's a fresh pot of coffee. Sit down and defrost. I'll take over the canopy," Adelaide offered.

The ornament tent had become so big that it needed its own staff member. This year, North Pole Evergreens expanded to a larger structure with three canvas sides to keep the wind out because they needed room for more tables for their Christmas merchandise. The first wall had a line of exterior greenery displays sitting on the ground, with a second row on a rough wooden bench behind them. They had been an unexpected hit last year, and their popularity had grown to the point where Victor had to refresh his supply every weekend.

Victor still had a table for ornaments along the opposite side, although this season her stained glass had equal billing with Victor's carvings. Last year, she'd sold enough to cover the cost of her supplies and to turn a small profit which she set aside for her future business, but her boyfriend had sold as many handmade ornaments as she did.

The protected table along the back wall was new this year, and it was dedicated to two editions of Aunt Addy's Activity Books: a Christmas edition and a nature edition. Adelaide beamed every time she saw them.

Victor had surprised her with a business card on the second night of last year's opening weekend. He told her that one of his customers was a printer, and that she should contact him to see if they could do her books. It took her until the new year to work up the courage to make the call. But it had been worth it.

Her dream was sitting in two stacks in front of her. The activity books were in magazine format, and each one was stuffed with puzzles, games, and jokes. Between what her stained glass earned her at the tree lot and at her craft shows last year, she'd saved enough to cover the printing costs of her first run of books. This fall, she sold out of her first printing at the local Christmas craft shows because her books had been a surprise hit as children's presents. In fact, she'd earned enough to do a second printing, as well as set aside some money to print two new editions in 1973. Then she'd really start turning a profit. Adelaide already had a list of campsite stores to visit the following spring to expand her reach.

"How are Aunt Addy's sales?"

"If this keeps up, my days at the bank could be numbered. I'll be too busy running my own empire to work for somebody else." That was the dream that she'd shared with Victor and her Thursday night businesswomen's group. "No more kisses. I have to get to work."

"Con is covering it. I need to talk to you about something." Victor took her shoulders and backed her up until she sat down on one of the kitchen table benches. "Owning a tree farm is not very traditional, but it's what I love and I'm making it work. Earning a living selling activity books isn't traditional either, but you are going to make it work. Our love of Christmas means that we work together really well, and I'd like to keep that going. But I think it's time that we moved our partnership into a new arena. A more permanent one."

He dropped to one knee in front of her. Victor fumbled a moment with the zipper on his ski jacket, but eventually got it open. He pulled out a small, square, black velvet box. "Would you like to be my partner in Christmas and everything else, Adelaide North, and do me the honour of marrying me?"

She gasped. Not only at the unexpected proposal but also at the unique engagement ring Victor was offering her. Instead of diamonds, it had a small ruby flanked by emerald chips, which was perfect for them. Their relationship had started at Christmas, and they'd kept up the same excitement and joy throughout the year. Adelaide didn't think that would ever change between them. "Victor Klassen, I would love to marry you."

He barely slipped the ring on her finger before he jumped to his feet and pulled Adelaide to hers. "You are the best Christmas present I could ever ask for. I love you, Adelaide North soon-to-be Klassen."

"I love you too, Victor." When she kissed him, she swore she tasted gingerbread.

"Do you think every Christmas will be this romantic?"

"I think that North Pole Evergreens and Aunt Addy's Activity Books are just getting started."

THE END

Keep reading for a special recipe featured in CHRISTMAS TREE CONNECTION

Coconut Christmas Trees

½ cup butter or margarine
2 cups icing (confectioner's) sugar
3 tbsp milk
3 cups unsweetened shredded coconut (medium or long strand)
½ tsp vanilla or mint flavoring
Green food coloring
4 oz white chocolate for melting (chopped up baking squares or wafers)

Melt butter or margarine in a large saucepan or microwave. Remove from heat if using stovetop. Add icing sugar and milk.

Mix in coconut and flavoring.

For trees: add enough green food coloring to tint mixture green.
For snowballs: do not add any coloring

Roll into 1" balls.

For trees: pinch tops to make into cones.
For snowballs: leave round.

Place in refrigerator, uncovered, for at least 4 hours – preferably overnight – to dry and firm.

Melt chocolate in saucepan or microwave. Dip tops of trees or snowballs to give make them "snow covered".

Makes about 3 dozen treats.

Elle's Notes

1. Be fancy and leave your trees "white", however the more yellow the butter or margarine is, the less white your trees will be. (I recommend a very pale butter if you want to try this.) They look great with brown chocolate topping (melted chocolate chips work fine.)

2. If you want to go retro, make pink Christmas trees (remember those?). Tint the coconut pink, add cherry flavoring instead of mint, and dip in white or regular brown chocolate.

3. Snowballs can be tinted any color.

If you enjoyed CHRISTMAS TREE CONNECTION, jingle all the way through the festive season with ELEVEN more novelettes that are like little bites of sweet and swoony delight.

These heartwarming and feel-good romances feature second chances, enemies turned lovers, fake dating adventures, and more, all wrapped up in the cozy merriment of the holidays. Plus, there's a cookie recipe in each book!

Find more on the Christmas Kisses and Cookie Crumbs series page on Amazon.

Read more about Adelaide and Victor! Forty years later, North Pole Unlimited has grown into a global, multi-generational empire, and romance continues to spread across December and the rest of Canada at Christmastime. Adelaide is handing over the reins of her Christmas company to her grandchildren, but she's keeping a hand in, especially when it comes to bringing love to one and all for the holidays. See what she's up to and meet a new group of Christmas romantics in DECKER AND JOY, the first North Pole Unlimited Sweet Christmas romance.

Here's a sneak peek at DECKER AND JOY...

Late October
   Ottawa, Ontario

A year after hanging out his shingle as a private investigator, his dream of being a private detective was dying a painful death. Decker Harkness needed an income-generating, career-making case if he wanted to keep the doors open, and he needed it yesterday. Strip-mall office rent was all he could afford, but he wouldn't even be able to manage that if things didn't pick up soon.

He didn't mind doing corporate security checks. They could be boring, but he was good at online investigations. Second best were the fraud cases his insurance-agent friends occasionally tossed his way. He was tired of the divorce and custody cases which paid most of his bills. They were beginning to permanently tarnish his view of humanity.

Which was why the email from North Pole Unlimited came at the perfect time. Decker had done a handful of jobs for NPU in the last year—employment checks on locals, tracking down owners of property they wanted to buy—but the message he received the day before hinted at a much bigger case. Proprietary technological information and potential corporate espionage were mentioned and set his heart racing. Decker had waited months for this kind of opportunity.

He pulled out one of his surviving suit jackets from his Ottawa Police Service days, and pressed his shirt and tie. He took a moment to check his fresh buzz cut in the mirror, and was pleased with how it hid the half-dozen silver hairs invading the brown at his temples. He looked ready to deal with a sensitive, classified problem for an international, multi-million-dollar company.

He'd even cleaned his office, sort of. He scanned the room one more time. His university diploma was visible on the wall behind him, as was his graduation picture from the police academy, and the photo of him getting his ten-year pin from the mayor. His office wasn't big, but he only did the parts the camera would catch.

It all looked good, except for the bald, lumbering black man who appeared outside his office door window holding two coffee cups. "Harkness, what are you doing in there? Open up!"

"Charlie? What's wrong?"

Charlie Barr had been his partner, first on patrol and later again when they'd worked together in Robbery. They'd kept in touch after Decker had left the force, but their run-ins had grown fewer and further between as their jobs pulled them in separate directions.

Decker unlocked the door and relieved Charlie of one of his cups before he cleared the threshold. "This is a surprise."

"But a surprise with coffee," Charlie said, his rough smoker's voice mangling the words.

"Which means you want something." He didn't mind.

"A sounding board. A new shoplifting ring has popped up with one of my sergeants. Get this. They use coupons," Charlie said.

"If they have coupons, it's not shoplifting."

"If they have legitimate coupons, it's not. This crew is printing and distributing them. Then, when the store is swamped with people wanting their freebies, they take their pick of the merchandise and walk out the door in all the confusion."

Why couldn't he have had this kind of case while he was still on the force? It was more challenging to catch thieves who used their brains instead of their brawn. Then he had a sip of the coffee Charlie had brought him, and remembered a perk of being self-employed: no more squad-room java. "That's incredibly low tech. Aren't they worried about security cameras?" Decker asked.

"When I say swamping the store, I mean close to a hundred shoppers descending at once. They target small stores where crowding is an issue."

"How can I help?" Charlie had shown up for some unofficial assistance, whether he admitted it or not. His old partner was a great cop, with an infallible ability to sniff out evidence, but his memory was horrible. Charlie had bought three copies of the same memory improvement book in the time they worked together, and he'd read them all.

"What was the name of the printer from that art gallery case we worked a few years ago? The one making the prints but wasn't legally complicit because they thought they had a contract? When was that?"

"Three years ago. Rainbow Ink. Wasn't it in your file notes?" As Charlie had said, the case had gone nowhere; no wonder he didn't recall the details.

"I didn't remember where I put them, and you were closer," Charlie said. "A cup of coffee is cheaper than asking the file clerk to pull everything."

Decker's computer beeped to signal the start of his video conference.

"I'll get out of your hair since you obviously have a date," Charlie teased.

"It's a business meeting. And at least I have hair," Decker countered.

"Well, if you're going to insult me, I'll leave." Charlie laughed on his way out. "Thanks for the help," he yelled as the door clicked shut.

When Decker answered the video call, he was surprised to see Nick Klassen at the other end of it. All his prior contracts with North Pole Unlimited originated with George Macintyre. When Nick explained that he was stepping in as the new vice-president of human resources, Decker offered his congratulations. "That's great. Please tell George to enjoy his retirement and go after all those fish he was talking about. I'm pleased that you thought of me. I hope we can continue working together."

His new employer nodded in agreement. "Me, too. This call wasn't just to inform you about George's retirement. As I mentioned in my email yesterday, I have a delicate situation that I need your help with."

Decker leaned closer to the screen, one hand gripping the pen he used to take notes. Nick might know who he was, but that didn't mean anything. Decker needed to prove himself all over again. He was up to the task; impressing a new—sort of new—client could lead to lots of work, and he needed every bit he could get if he wanted his business to stay afloat. There was no case too big or small for Harkness investigations.

Although this one was definitely on the small side. "You want me to find a doll?" Decker repeated for the third time. "An E.L.V.I.S. doll?" His alarm bells were clanging; the case couldn't be as easy as Nick was presenting it as.

"It's a prototype," Nick explained. "A very expensive one. It has some animatronic components and some recording playback devices that aren't ready for consumer use, which is why we need it back. We've been working on this project for years as a replacement for an existing product. E.L.V.I.S. accidentally went to a store in your area which sells our Funster pet toy line. Unfortunately, we aren't certain which location it was shipped to. I'm going to send you a list. We need you to visit the stores, find it, and retrieve it at any cost. The unit has a GPS chip installed. That should help you."

"Why can't you track it with the GPS?" Decker asked. He wanted the business, but this was basically running an errand. It wasn't the stepping stone to bigger, more important cases he'd hoped for from NPU. If anything, it was a demotion. But if the situation were as insignificant as it seemed, why would a vice-president be involved? Something was fishy about the entire setup.

"The chip is currently on the fritz. It broadcasts, but only on an extremely limited range. That's one of the kinks we need to work out. E.L.V.I.S. can't be running around in the wild, Decker. I cannot emphasize how important it is to get it back to our labs as soon as possible. Can you handle this?" The blond giant leaned into the lens on his computer. "You'll have a week to find E.L.V.I.S. We can't give you any longer."

A week to recover a doll? Now Decker was insulted, but he didn't let it show. "No problem," he assured the man on the screen. The job wasn't what he'd thought it would be, but it was one less cheating spouse he'd have to follow. And recovering private property was a legitimate job.

"Excellent. We've sent an encrypted email to your account. My assistant Jilly will text you the security password. We'll include a picture and some of the specs for you. There will also be a link to the GPS tracker and a list of the stores where it might have been sent. I'll expect daily progress reports, Decker. Again, I cannot emphasize how dangerous this can be in the wrong hands. Good luck." The screen went dead.

It was a doll. How much trouble could it be?

The email arrived in his inbox moments after he shut down the video link. Decker spent the rest of the morning studying the file. The prototype looked like G.I. Joe and Malibu Ken had a secret love child. The figure in the photo had a black, plastic pompadour and a shiny utility belt over its navy ninja suit. Decker didn't have children, but he didn't see it appealing to boys or to girls. Then again, he didn't have to play with it. He just had to find it.

The GPS app which Nick's assistant sent was simple to use. Unfortunately, the results were inconclusive. It displayed a large circle around Archer Plaza, a two-story shopping center off the Queensway, before flashing an error message and dying. Decker couldn't tell if the problem was with the app or E.L.V.I.S. Three of the possible locations on Decker's list were in that area. It was convenient for narrowing his search, but it meant he had to brave a mall. A week before Halloween. And the night before, he'd seen a news segment about how some stores were already putting up Christmas decorations. E.L.V.I.S.'s timing was terrible.

He started the search as soon as the mall opened the next morning. Nothing impressed clients like fast results.

His first stop was equally inoffensive and unmemorable. Fins and Things was a small store specializing in terrariums and aquariums, and in the fish, lizards, and snakes to fill them. It only had a small bin of toys for other animals. Their biweekly supply order arrived while Decker was in the store, and when they checked the box in front of him, they came up empty. They were definitely off his list.

He hesitated outside Kitten Caboodle, another store on the mall's main level. Decker peered through the window and was impressed with what he saw. A private animal shelter and adoption center took up half the space; the rest was a fully stocked pet store. This was a place pets and owners would appreciate. Bright, clean, well laid out. He spotted a full aisle of toys running the length of the store, and that didn't include the stuffed animals tucked among the other merchandise.

Kitten Caboodle was a contender.

❄

"Oh, thank you, delivery fairies!" Joy McCall clapped her hands together at the sight of the man wheeling a trolley through the front doors of Kitten Caboodle. She refrained from jumping in deference to the orange kitten on her shoulder. Its little claws were dug in tightly to her navy knit cardigan, but the little thing wasn't strong enough to withstand that level of shaking.

Joy plucked the cat from her top and set it in the glass-sided display box which acted like a playpen. "In you go, Pumpkin." The kitten toddled toward the pile of napping fluff balls in the corner. He immediately snuggled with the three nearly identical black brothers who were even tinier than he was. Spooky, Midnight, and Stinky Spice, like Pumpkin, had two speeds: espresso high and asleep. Joy was grateful for the temporary break. It had been kitten-palooza lately.

A pair of teenagers had found Pumpkin near an apartment complex by the mall. Joy offered to hand-feed him until he was fully weaned. A few days later, a pregnant black cat had been left in a box at the shelter's back door. The poor thing had been in bad shape but still managed to deliver three healthy kittens before she passed away, and Joy volunteered for more foster kitten duty.

It was a twenty-four-hour-a-day job, and had taken a month, but Joy and the cats had survived all the late-night feedings. Fortunately, working in a shelter meant Joy could keep them in the store during her shifts and bundle them up in a carrier for the trips back and forth to her apartment.

After making sure the kittens were settled for the moment, Joy helped unload the boxes full of goodies. Once she signed for them, she was left with four cases of the newest Funsters from North Pole Unlimited's online catalogue. "Okay, listen up," she said. The store was empty except for the animals in it. "These toys are for paying customers. No knocking them off shelves. No chewing on the packaging. No playing with them. Paws off."

Mitzi, the miniature schnauzer Kitten Caboodle had temporarily taken in while her owner was hospitalized, lifted her head from her doggie bed and yawned in Joy's direction. "Excellent. Good job paying attention, everybody. I should have prefaced that with T-R-E…" All heads in the shop were turned in her direction by the second letter of the word treats. "That's all I am to you, isn't it? Your personal chef. Fine. I'll remember this," Joy muttered as she began pulling the boxes behind the counter. "You'd miss me if I left."

The store went silent, and Joy wished she could take it back. But it was true. After years of applying for local veterinary assistant positions, she'd taken the plunge and registered with an employment agency. They hadn't got back to her yet, but Joy was ever-hopeful that she would find a job in the area.

Something that would give her a bump in pay so she could get a bigger place. Maybe even a house someday. Until a few weeks ago, she hadn't considered the possibility of owning cats, not where she was currently living. It was next to impossible to find an apartment that would take one pet, let alone four. She needed to find her boys forever homes, but for the moment, Joy was burying her head in the sand.

She wouldn't give up the ungrateful beasts to just anyone, which was why Kitten Caboodle ran background checks on their customers before they left the shelter with an animal. Every soul in the store went home with an award-winning human. Joy couldn't keep all their rescue animals, no matter how much she wanted to, so she did her best to make sure they got the best of everything.

That included toys, and NPU products were top notch. The company's stuffed animals were tear-resistant, and their iron-hide chew toys lasted forever. "Oh, you guys should see the new stuff," she told them. Joy quickly sorted and shelved the contents of the first two crates, taking a moment to cuddle the fluffy lions and tigers. Another indicator of NPU's quality was that they didn't mess around when they shipped things. There was a hole torn in the bottom of the third container, but it looked to have been resealed with packing tape. None the contents listed on the invoice were missing. North Pole Unlimited was a quality outfit all the way around.

Joy was transferring the last of the catnip-stuffed mice into the bin with the latching, pet-proof lid when the dark-haired man who had been staring through the window for the last five minutes finally made his move.

He was cute. Clean-cut. Well-dressed for a casual outfit. His khakis and forest green shirt were nearly new. He didn't have a jacket, but he didn't need one for the unseasonably mild late-October weather. Joy didn't realize how tall he was until he got closer. Her eyes were level with the dimple he had at the side of his mouth. "Hi," she said.

He stared at her for a second and squinted at the nametag on her chest. "Hello, Joy. I'm Decker."

"Hi, Decker. Can I help you today?"

"I truly hope so. Do you have any Funsters? It's a line of pet toys."

It was an odd request; customers never asked for toys by brand. "Absolutely. Almost a whole aisle full, in fact. Are you looking for anything in particular? Who for? Cat? Small dog?

Big dog?" He looked like the big dog type. Not a Rottweiler or pit bull. Maybe a husky.

"I'm looking for a doll. About this big." He held his hands a foot apart. "It has dark clothes and it moves. Kind of like an army action figure."

"I didn't know Funsters came as dolls. I can tell you we don't have any." Human-shaped animal toys were never a big seller.

He shook his head insistently. "I happen to know NPU accidentally sent one to a store in the area. Kitten Caboodle was on their list. I really need to find that doll. Can you please double-check your stock?" Decker asked. He took off his Senators cap, as if it would make him appear more earnest.

It worked. The poor fellow looked as disappointed as he sounded. At the rate he was wringing his cap brim, it was going to be a perfect circle by the end of the day. "I think there might be a little left to sort through in this last box," she relented.

Decker leaned over her shoulder as she emptied the last carton. He smelled like—she inhaled again—sugar cookies. An unusual scent for a man, but it worked for him.

"Lions and tigers and bears. Nothing else," she said. "Sorry, no doll. I can keep my eyes open if you'd like."

His frown didn't last long, but Joy knew she saw it. "That's okay. Thanks for looking. Maybe I'll check out your store for a bit," he said.

"Let me know if you need help."

She kept an eye on him as he perused everything. *Everything.* He didn't seem to have a preference for either cat or dog items. And the man was not afraid to get dirty. Although he had to be six feet tall, he went up on his toes to search the back of the top shelves. Then he knelt to see everything she had on the floor, which was bags of dog food and kitty litter.

"Are you looking for anything in particular? Aside from the doll?" Joy asked as he moved to the last row.

"No."

As he bent to check the bottom shelf, Joy noticed Pumpkin had abandoned his nap in favour of the new plaything in front of him. She wasn't sure how the cat had managed to get up to the top of the playpen's glass wall, but the kitten was wobbling on the narrow wooden edge.

Then he launched.

Pumpkin's little legs splayed out. The fur ball didn't get much lift or distance from his pathetic jump. He just fell. Luckily for him, Decker's back made the drop only a foot.

Unluckily for Decker, the fleece he was wearing looked thicker than it apparently was.

"Yeow!"

Joy wasn't sure if the scream came from the man or the cat.

ALSO BY ELLE RUSH

SWEET CONTEMPORARY ROMANCE

North Pole Unlimited

Decker and Joy

Hollis and Ivy

Nick and Eve

Rudy and Kris

Ben and Jilly

Frank and Ginger

Noel and Merrily

Hopewell Millionaires

Doctor Millionaire

Fall a Million Times

A Million Love Notes

Royal Oak Ranch

The Cowboy and the Movie Star

The Cowboy and the Pastry Princess

The Cowboy and the Constable

The Cowgirl and the Duke (coming soon)

Holiday Beach (also available in print)

Shamrocks and Surprises

Pumpkins and Promises

Tinsel and Teacups

Fireworks and Frenemies

Birthdays and Bachelors

North Pole Unlimited Collection (also available in print)

Collection 1 - Decker and Joy, Hollis and Ivy

Collection 2 - Nick and Eve, Rudy and Kris

Collection 3 - Ben and Jilly, Frank and Ginger

Resort Romances

Cuban Moon

Mexican Sunsets

Dominican Stars

Mayan Midnights

Complete series 4-book box set

COOKBOOKS
Heartmade Collection

Brunch

Mains and Sides

Holiday Table

ABOUT THE AUTHOR

Elle Rush is a contemporary romance author from Winnipeg, Manitoba, Canada. When she's not travelling, she's hard at work writing books which are set all over the world. From Hollywood to the house next door, her heroes will make you swoon and her heroines will have you laughing out loud.

Elle has a degree in Spanish and French, barely passed German, and has flunked poetry in every language she ever studied, including English. She also has mild addictions to tea, yarn, bad sci-fi movies, and her garden.

Keep up with Elle's updates and new releases by subscribing to her newsletter.

Made in United States
Troutdale, OR
11/13/2024

24751306R10043